Deborah Kotter

Arnold
Always Answers

Pictures by Jane Conteh-Morgan

A Doubleday Book for Young Readers

A Doubleday Book for Young Readers
Published by
Delacorte Press
Bantam Doubleday Dell Publishing Group, Inc.
1540 Broadway
New York, New York 10036
Doubleday and the portrayal of an anchor with a dolphin are trademarks of
Bantam Doubleday Dell Publishing Group, Inc.
Text copyright © 1993 by Deborah Kotter
Illustrations copyright © 1993 by Jane Conteh-Morgan

Library of Congress Cataloging in Publication Data
Kotter, Deborah.
Arnold always answers / by Deborah Kotter ;
pictures by Jane Conteh-Morgan.
p.   cm.
Summary: Arnold enjoys a day of play with his mother.
ISBN 0-385-30905-8
[1. Mothers and sons—Fiction.   2. Play—Fiction.]   I. Conteh-Morgan, Jane, ill.
II. Title.
PZ7.K8546Ar   1993   [E]—dc20   92-18578   CIP   AC

Manufactured in Hong Kong
September 1993
10 9 8 7 6 5 4 3 2 1
SCP

Happy Reading!

Deborah Kotter

"Awake or asleep?"
Mother asked.
"Awake!"
Arnold jumped out of bed.

"Down or up?"
Mother asked.
"Down."
Arnold walked down the stairs.

"Hot or cold?"
"Hot."
Arnold ate hot oatmeal.

"Long or short?"
"Long."
Arnold pulled on long pants.

"In or out?"
"Out."
Arnold ran out to play.

"High or low?"
"High."
Mother pushed Arnold high
in the swing.

"More playtime,"
Arnold said.
"No, rest time,"
said Mother.

"Fast or slow?"
Mother asked.
"Fast!"
Arnold raced down the path
and fell into a mud puddle.

"Laugh or cry?"
"Cry."
But Arnold laughed!

"Dirty or clean?"
"Dirty."
Arnold looked at
his pants and shoes.

"Big or little?"
"Big."
Arnold played big fish
in the bathtub.

"Black or white?"
"Black."
Arnold took Black Bear to bed.

"Hugs or kisses?"
Mother asked.
"Both!"
Arnold hugged
and kissed his mother.
Mother hugged
and kissed Arnold.